nickelodeon

TEENAGE MUTANT NINJA™ TURTLES

THE BIG BOOK OF NINJA TURTLES

A GOLDEN BOOK · NEW YORK

© 2014 Viacom International Inc. and Viacom Overseas Holdings C.V. All rights reserved. Published in the United States by Golden Books, an imprint of Random House Children's Books, a division of Random House LLC, 1745 Broadway, New York, NY 10019, and in Canada by Random House of Canada Limited, Toronto, Penguin Random House Companies. Golden Books, A Golden Book, A Big Golden Book, the G colophon, and the distinctive gold spine are registered trademarks of Random House LLC. Nickelodeon, Teenage Mutant Ninja Turtles, and all related titles, logos, and characters are trademarks of Viacom International Inc. and Viacom Overseas Holdings C.V. Based on characters created by Peter Laird and Kevin Eastman.

ISBN 978-0-553-50769-0
randomhouse.com/kids
Printed in the United States of America
10 9 8 7 6 5 4 3

THE WORLD OF THE NINJA

Ninjas are cunning martial arts masters. They use strength, weapons, and intelligence to complete their missions.

Ninjas outthink their enemies. They use their environment to their advantage. A ninja makes no unnecessary movements and wastes no words.

A true ninja does not receive awards or recognition, because he or she is secretive. Hiding in the sewers of New York City are four very special ninjas and their master.

They are mutants. They are green. They are brothers.

LEONARDO
THE LEADER

Serious and dedicated, Leonardo is the leader of the Turtles. He trains constantly, hoping to become the ideal martial artist. Unfortunately, for the moment, he's an inexperienced teen with three smart-aleck brothers, which often leaves him feeling frustrated.

Donatello is the team's brilliant inventor. He can make amazing gadgets, weapons, and vehicles with items scavenged from the trash. Donatello likes order and logic, and he can't stand it when his brothers mess with his stuff.

DONATELLO
THE INVENTOR

Raphael is the biggest and toughest of the Turtles. He doesn't have time for stealth—he'd rather meet a foe head-on. Raphael might question his brothers' plans and tactics, but he's always ready to fight for them.

RAPHAEL
THE WARRIOR

MICHELANGELO
THE JOKESTER

The youngest and most energetic of the Turtles, Michelangelo is also the friendliest and most lighthearted. He'd rather solve a problem with a joke than with a fight.

SPLINTER

Splinter is the Turtles' sensei, or teacher. Having lost his wife and daughter, he is determined to train and protect his new family. He is a master ninja, and his Zen philosophy sometimes baffles the Turtles.

ICE CREAM KITTY

This frosty feline is a mutant combination of house cat and ice cream. Her body is made of strawberry, chocolate, and vanilla ice cream, and her claws are very sharp. Michelangelo keeps her in the Turtles' freezer.

THE LAIR

The lair is the Turtles' underground hideaway. Built in an abandoned subway terminal, it is their home and headquarters. Each Turtle has his own room, but there is also a common room, where they can come together to watch television, play video games, and best of all, eat pizza.

THE DOJO

The *dojo* is the combined gym and classroom where Leonardo, Michelangelo, Raphael, and Donatello train to be ninjas. With Splinter as their sensei, they practice martial arts, defensive tactics, offensive strikes, and Zen philosophy.

WEAPONS

Michelangelo's weapons of choice are *nunchucks*. These two hard sticks connected by a chain can be spun to deliver a striking blow, or they can be used defensively.

Leonardo is skilled with his *katanas*, which are sharp, finely crafted steel swords. He can wield two at the same time as if they were one blade.

Though Donatello can make any weapon he wants, nothing compares to his *bo* staff. This is a long stick with a blade at the end.

Raphael's *sai* is a long blade with sharp prongs on either side. He can use it to block an enemy's attack or to make a point of his own.

SHELLRAISER

Built from scavenged parts and an old subway car, this armored assault vehicle is the Turtles' ultimate weapon. It can travel on city streets and subway tracks. Inside the van, Leonardo drives, Raphael handles the weapons, Michelangelo navigates, and Donatello is the chief engineer.

MANHOLE-COVER LAUNCHER

STEALTH BIKE DEPLOYMENT

TRASH CANNON

SHELLRAISER

STEAMROLLER AND CLAWS

STEALTH BIKE

Hidden inside the *Shellraiser*, Raphael's three-wheeled chopper deploys a shell-shaped shield that allows it to blend perfectly with the pavement. Its electric motor runs silently to avoid detection.

PATROL BUGGY

This four-man dune buggy splits into four separate go-karts, one for each of the Turtles. It is ideal for driving through narrow alleys and crowded city streets.

APRIL O'NEIL

This sixteen-year-old girl is on a mission to find her father, a scientist who was captured by the Kraang. Her friends the Turtles have vowed to help her. Splinter is teaching her to become a *kunoichi*, a female ninja.

CASEY JONES

This teenage vigilante is a good friend of the Turtles. He loves to play hockey and he loves to fight crime. He's a skilled but untrained martial artist who can sometimes be hotheaded and arrogant.

KRAANG

The Kraang are brainlike invaders from another dimension. Because their home is becoming uninhabitable, they are trying to transform Earth's environment into one suitable for them. They use the offices of the mysterious company TCRI as their headquarters.

MUTAGEN

The Kraang's main weapon is a powerful chemical mutagen sometimes called ooze. A little drop can mutate anything it touches. It can make normal creatures bigger and stronger, and it can combine the DNA of different species to make completely new beings.

KRAANG-DROID

The Kraang occupy android hosts that enable them to perform day-to-day activities. They can walk, talk, fight, and even eat.

SHREDDER

Shredder, also known as Oroku Saki, is a powerful martial arts master and a fierce underworld boss. Hidden behind armor of metal blades, he works to destroy Splinter and the Ninja Turtles.

KARAI

Karai is a cunning and strong-willed *kunoichi*. She is very loyal to her teacher and adoptive father, Shredder.

THE FOOT CLAN

Shredder leads a vast army of ninja warriors known as the Foot Clan. Originally from Japan, they are fearless and obey him without question.

FOOTBOTS

The Kraang created these robotic warriors and gave them to Shredder to help him destroy the Turtles. With a rotating saw and a giant blade for hands, they are dangerous and deadly.

BAXTER STOCKMAN

This bumbling scientist is an enemy of the Turtles. His inventions have also aided Shredder and the Purple Dragon gang. The Turtles like to annoy Baxter by getting his name wrong.

MOUSERS

These Mobile Offensive Underground Search Excavation and Retrieval Sentries are small robots designed by Baxter Stockman. Their size makes them ideal for stealing from banks, power stations, and other secure areas.

DOGPOUND

Chris Bradford was an arrogant martial arts star and a student of the evil ninja master, Shredder. But a dog bite and a splash of mutagen changed him into Dogpound. He's a powerful enemy of the Turtles and remains loyal to Shredder.

RAHZAR

During a battle with Mikey, Dogpound fell into a giant vat of mutagen. The result was a bigger, stronger, more mutated monster called Rahzar. He has long fangs, massive metallic claws and spikes, and a protective exoskeleton.

FISHFACE

Xever was a low-level thug until Shredder plucked him out of prison to do his bidding. After being exposed to a mutagen bomb, he became Fishface, a mutant with a poisonous bite. Baxter Stockman built him robot legs and a breathing device so he can continue to track down and battle the Turtles.

SNAKEWEED

Snake was a common thug until he was splashed by some mutagen during a fight with the Turtles. His DNA combined with that of a plant, and he grew to nearly thirty feet! The Turtles destroyed him once, but weeds have a habit of popping up again and again. . . .

THE RAT KING

Dr. Victor Falco was a ruthless scientist who teamed up with the Kraang. He used their mutagen to create a serum that enabled psychic powers. He tested it on himself and became a giant human/rat hybrid who can telepathically control rats. No rat mind—not even Splinter's—is safe from his powers.

LEATHERHEAD

This powerful mutant started life as a normal alligator, but he was flushed down the toilet and captured by the Kraang. Before he could escape, they experimented on him, making him large, strong, and very angry.

His martial arts skills aren't as developed as the Turtles', but his incredible strength makes him a powerful ally in the Turtles' fight against the Kraang. He really likes Michelangelo's Pizza Noodle Soup.

PIGEON PETE

While developing mutagen, the Kraang experimented on dozens of animals and humans. Pete is the result of one of these experiments. His combined pigeon and human DNA allows him to fly and speak. Though he's excitable and has a short attention span, he can be helpful to the Turtles.

KIRBY BAT

The Turtles' friend April O'Neil was in danger of being hit with mutagen, but her father, Kirby, pushed her out of the way—and got splashed himself. He became Kirby Bat, a giant red-bearded, middle-aged bat.

MAD MONKEY

Dr. Tyler Rockwell was a brilliant scientist who was changed into a giant monkey by his devious partner, Dr. Falco. He retained much of his intelligence but developed telepathic powers.

NEWTRALIZER

Accidentally released from a Kraang prison by Donnie, the Newtralizer is a large reptilian creature loaded with weapons, including lasers, missiles, saw blades, and mines. Though he's an enemy of the Kraang, he doesn't like the Turtles much either.

MUTAGEN MAN

When Tim, a mild-mannered ice cream vendor, first saw the Turtles in action, he knew he wanted to be a crime fighter. So he made himself a costume and became the Pulverizer. During a battle with Dogpound, he doused himself with mutagen, hoping to gain super strength. Instead, he became Mutagen Man, a strange blob with an acidic touch.

TIGER CLAW

This bounty hunter from Japan is a tiger/human hybrid. He began life as a circus performer, but after being mutated, he became one of Shredder's most dreaded henchmen. Tiger Claw lost his tail in a battle and has been hunting the soldier who took it ever since.

PARASITICA

Another Kraang mutagen experiment gone bad, this enormous parasitic wasp has the power to brainwash its victims with a simple sting.

COCKROACH TERMINATOR

When Donnie outfitted a common cockroach with surveillance gear to spy on the Kraang, it seemed like a great idea—until the bug fell into a vat of mutagen. Now he's a giant mechanized monster who's gone rogue. This really bothers Raph because he has a fear of cockroaches.

SQUIRRELANOIDS

These are not your average cute and fuzzy squirrels. Mutagen has made them big, strong, and vicious. They multiply in people's stomachs, grow quickly, and *love* popcorn. Mikey's knowledge of comic-book monsters comes in handy when the Turtles are fighting these nutty nightmares.

SPIDER-BYTEZ

This spider/human hybrid was originally a rude New Yorker named Vic. He didn't like the Turtles, or as he called them, the "Kung-Fu Frogs." During a fight with the Kraang, some mutagen splattered on him. He transformed into Spider-Bytez, a mean-spirited mutant with increased strength who can spit acid and shoot super-strong webs.

TURTLE POWER!

The streets of New York City are filled with mystery, mutants, and adventure, so Leonardo, Michelangelo, Raphael, and Donatello are always working together to fight for good and protect their friends.